FAR ENOUGH

A WESTERN IN FRAGMENTS

Also by Joe Wilkins

Memoir

The Mountain and the Fathers: Growing up on the Big Dry

Poetry

Notes from the Journey Westward

Killing the Murnion Dogs

Chapbooks

Leviathan

We Had to Go On Living

Ragged Point Road

As Editor

The Far Edges of the Fourth Genre: An Anthology of Explorations in Creative Nonfiction

FAR ENOUGH

A WESTERN IN FRAGMENTS

Joe Wilkins

Black
Lawrence
Press

Black Lawrence Press
www.blacklawrence.com

Executive Editor: Diane Goettel
Chapbook Editor: Kit Frick
Book and cover design: Amy Freels

ISBN: 978-1-62557-994-2

Published 2015 by Black Lawrence Press.
Printed in the United States.

Thanks to Elizabeth Quinn for publishing an earlier version of Far Enough *in* High Desert Journal. *Thanks as well to Mary Clearman Blew—for the vision in the first place.*

This one's for Edie, my little sweetie.

Winter-born

Willie Benson lost his right thumb at the Newman branding in the spring of '92, the ninth year of drought along the Musselshell River Valley. He was roping calves and accidentally headed a big, winter-born Angus. The calf jerked hard on the rope, eyes going wide and white. Willie braced down on the saddle horn and dallied up quick but caught his thumb just under the knuckle. Days later, sprawled on a chair at the Ryegate Bar, Willie told his friends he felt rope grind hard down on bone. He said his horse reared back, the calf's tongue lolled out—*and my goddamn thumb popped clean off.*

About the Blood

Wade Newman, Willie's boss and owner of the RL Ranch, the biggest spread of private land all down the river, knew the work day was done. He had thought they might finish his fifteen hundred head of calves in just three days, but once they got Willie loaded into the cab of someone's pickup and sent off to the hospital, the cowboys started passing a fifth of whiskey. It wasn't even late afternoon, the sky wide and hot with dust. But Wade figured they might as well open up the beer coolers and put on the steaks. He knew Willie's thumb would be the big story tonight at the Ryegate Bar, and as he flung hunks of meat to the fire, he thought about how he'd tell it, the loud bawl of that heavy calf and the rope's sudden, rip-tight twang. He took a cold drink of beer. He'd tell about the blood.

Next Time

Willie Benson was only twenty when he lost his thumb and not legal to drink, but Wade Newman handed him a bottle of Jim Beam as they left the hospital anyway. Willie got drunk quick and stayed that way most of the week. Pulling into the gravel lot next to the Ryegate Bar, Wade waved down Tim Dejagher, the county sheriff. He slipped Dejagher a fifty and told him Willie and his buddies were going to have a bit of a party, just cut loose and not bother anybody. Dejagher nodded and leaned further into the open window. He pointed at Willie's bandaged hand, told him he was glad to hear it was just a thumb. Then a grin broke over Dejagher's thick face—*but watch out, Willie, it might be your pecker next time!*

Free Beers until Midnight

Wade Newman paid for everything at the Ryegate Bar the night of Willie Benson's party. He had Russ Crandall, who owned the place, grilling out back and Edna, Russ's wife, pouring free beers until midnight. Wade sat up at the bar, sipping bourbon. He rested his elbows on the lacquered pine, his boots on the brass rail below. He watched Willie, who was leaned back in a plastic chair at an old wood table over by the poker machines. He saw Willie's thin legs scattered underneath him, his right arm tight at his chest in a sling, his left arm lying across the carved up tabletop in a puddle of beer. Wade could see Willie's head move in slow, drunken circles, and he wondered how Willie felt about the whole deal, if he had room to feel with all that booze on his brain. He watched Willie swing his left arm out from the pivot of his shoulders, grab a glass of beer, and take a long, hard drink.

The Night's Freeze

Willie Benson's father, Dean Benson, had been a full-time poker player and sometime logger. In the winter of '88, behind in a big game of stud at Two Dot, he started hauling logs out of the mountains north of the valley in early February. One morning before sunup, hungover from a long night at the Ryegate Bar, Dean worked his way to a ridge above a dry creek. The wind was cold, blowing hard scrims of snow across the ground, and Dean set a cut wrong and dropped a pine across his back. Tim Dejagher found him three days later, stiff and blue with the night's freeze. Daisy Benson, Willie's mother, cried hysterically between drags of her cigarette at the funeral, then moved down to Billings to take a job serving drinks at Tracy's Trucker Lounge. Willie, in the middle of his junior year, knowing there wasn't any room for him in the apartment above Tracy's, stayed with the Newmans and told folks it was so he could finish at Ryegate High School. Wade had never thought much of the Bensons, but he liked Willie's polite and thoughtful answers to his questions and so taught the boy to rope and ride and gave him a room in the main house, even had him take his meals with the family. Wade's wife, Vera, started hauling Willie to Congregational Church services on Sunday and picking up library books for him when she went into Harlowton for groceries. Willie did what he could for the Newmans in return: cutting grass in the summer, shoveling the walk on winter mornings, cowboying for Wade on the weekends. He even showed Jackie, Wade and Vera's only child, how to gut a trout on her twelfth birthday.

A Summer without Rain

Wade Newman wasn't supposed to get the RL. He was the youngest of three brothers, and Robert Newman, Wade's father, had wanted to give the ranch to the oldest of his boys, Franklin. But in the spring of '83 the drought hit, and Franklin Newman got religion. When his father asked if he wanted to take over the RL, Franklin told him a summer without rain was a sign. He said he saw calf blood washed across the rimrocks riding home one evening, said the locusts were next—*and Daddy, I don't want any piece of earth keeping me from heaven.* Robert Newman stared hard at his oldest son, then told him he could either start praying for rain or pack up and go shovel shit for a living for all he cared. Franklin Newman left that evening. Junior Newman was Robert's next oldest, but he'd broke his neck riding bulls at the Brockton Rodeo years back and spent most of his days drinking cola through a straw and watching soap operas on the television in the front room of the main house. So, after running the biggest ranch along the Musselshell for nearly sixty years, and even though Wade spent too much time at the Ryegate Bar and not enough time fixing fence, Robert turned the RL over to his youngest son. Wade and Vera moved into the main house, the river dried, and two months later, while Wade took his lunch in town, Robert Newman died sitting in an easy chair.

The Way the Wind Stacks the Snow in the Pines

Caleb Meyer ate lunch at the Ryegate Bar the first Friday of the month right at noon. He ordered the same thing each visit: hamburger steak with grilled onions and mashed potatoes and gravy. His beard was thick as a magpie's nest, and he smelled of vinegar and sheep. He lived up north, almost a day's ride, near the foothills of the Snowy Mountains. No one knew how long Meyer had been around or if he had any family. Wade Newman, who liked to watch Russ nod in agreement as he catalogued the people of Ryegate and their ancestry, christened Meyer the official town derelict. But during his senior year in high school, Willie Benson cut fourth period class every Friday that Meyer was in town. Willie would come down to the bar where Meyer told him stories about tracking bobcat along Bascom Creek, the way the wind stacks the snow in the pines, or how the mountains drove his mother mad. When they were doing fiction in senior English, Willie wrote down the one about Caleb's mother and the mountains. He got an A, and, at the top of his paper, his teacher wrote—*Beautiful!*

A Damn Fine Cowboy

Willie Benson had told Wade and Vera that after he graduated he wanted to go to the vo-tech school over in Great Falls, learn to be a lineman—*make some money with the power company, maybe buy a little place up there and help my mom out.* Vera smiled, told him that was sweet and honorable and that a lineman was a fine occupation for a young man. But Wade shook his head. Cattle prices were down and the rain still hadn't come and Wade was worried about the ranch. He told Willie he couldn't let him go—*you're a damn fine cowboy, and I need you on the RL a few more years, Willie, at least until the drought breaks.* So when Willie graduated from high school, he moved out into the bunkhouse with the other cowboys, and the day after Willie lost his thumb, before the doctors checked him out and Wade picked him up to go to the Ryegate Bar, Willie called the technical school in Great Falls. They told him a guy had to have two thumbs to hang on a power pole—*Sorry.*

River Bottom

Jackie Newman didn't feel right about Willie Benson. She turned fifteen the day she watched them haul Willie, all bloody-armed and bawling, from off his horse and into the cab of someone's truck for the ride to the hospital. She was out of school for the summer now, helping her mom cook for the cowboys who didn't take their meals at the Ryegate Bar, and it was Willie's first day up and around after his party, after all the booze. Still not used to eating with his left hand, he kept fumbling his fork, and the other cowboys called him Stumpy and laughed. Jackie walked back into the kitchen. She didn't want to hear their laughs that sounded like tires grabbing gravel, didn't want to see the chuckle and shake in their long bony necks. She tossed her apron on the counter and ran down to the barn. She saddled her horse and rode to the river where she found a hole of water that hadn't yet dried. Jackie stripped off her t-shirt and jeans and stepped into the river and lay down, letting the warm mud and water ooze around her shoulders and hips, down her legs. When Willie came home with A's on his papers, Jackie's mom made him read them to the whole family. Jackie loved the one about the woman all alone up in the mountains. She loved how the mountain creeks ran cool and clear, how trout fought the swift water. She had lived in the valley all her life and never imagined the world could be that way. And with the Musselshell so low each spring, she hadn't caught a trout in almost two years. She reached her hands down to the river bottom and pulled up great handfuls of black mud.

Dreaming Rain

Wade Newman rode west as the horizon drank the spill of sun from the sky. The wind blew dust across his face, into his eyes. He held up an arm to see and dreamed for a moment that the dust was rain. The hard skin and meaty flesh around his eyes and mouth curved into a smile. He hoped Vera was cooking lamb chops and fried potatoes. He figured he'd make a trip into the Ryegate Bar after dinner and have a beer. He thought Willie might finally be sobered up and feeling better about the whole thing and ready to break some horses soon. So Wade Newman rode for home, smiling, dreaming rain and a fast running river, dreaming lamb chops and green broke horses. And the dust beat against his face.

Shade of a Jackpine

Willie Benson drove the fencing truck—a yellow, banged-up Chevy Luv—toward the wheat fields out on the high plains to the north. He bumped over the dirt road, dust rising from beneath his tires, and smelled the heat of the day coming on, the dry pastureland about him studded with pear cactus and sagebrush. Willie didn't mind fixing fence, but he knew Wade had sent him out here to get him away from the other cowboys, away from their jeers and trips to the Ryegate Bar as soon as the work day was done. Wheat never wandered through holes in the fence, and Wade seldom ran cattle out in these pastures. As the dust settled around the stopped Chevy, Willie could see no one had bothered to keep up this fence at all, old and ragged as it was, the wires brittle with rust, rotten pine posts leaning like loose teeth. But Willie worked all morning anyway, pounding steel posts and stretching new wire. In the heat of the day, with most of the work behind him, he napped in the shade of a jackpine and woke as the evening shadows strung themselves across the prairie. The bandage on his hand itched something terrible. He fished his whiskey flask from his pocket and took a drink. He stared at the mountains, the huge and shadowed Snowies. Though Willie knew they were at least a day's ride away, they looked so close, like maybe he could start running and be halfway up in a couple of minutes.

Smile Anyway

Jackie Newman scrambled up the wooden ring of the corral and sat on the top rung. She pulled an apple from her pocket and ate it slowly. It was sweet and cold. To the north, she could see the rimrocks rise up from the valley floor, and beyond the rimrocks the far blue shimmer of the Snowy Mountains. Now the old Chevy Luv came racing down the dirt road, throwing great arcs of dust across the sun, and everything Jackie saw—the gray corral boards, the craggy bark of the cottonwoods, her own hands—went a reddish shade of gold. She knew it was just Willie Benson on his way to the Ryegate Bar, but the surprise of color made her smile anyway. She watched for a moment, then winged the last of her apple to the dusty sky.

Plain Angry

Wade Newman gave Willie Benson a raise a month after the accident. Vera made him do it. She told him Willie was depressed—*he's only twenty-years-old and already drinking, already driving the same road his no-account Daddy walked*—and Vera's solution to Willie's troubles was a raise to show the boy what he was worth. Wade wasn't so sure. Willie had been a top hand before—better with a lariat than most of the other cowboys, and smarter too. Wade had even daydreamed a time or two about training the boy up as his foreman. But it seemed like Willie didn't much care about getting the job done right anymore. Wade sat in his office, sat up at the big pine desk his daddy had built and shuffled receipts, tried to work out the balances. But he was always punching the wrong numbers into the adding machine and losing track of the year's diesel bill or feed for the cowboy's horses or the price of barbed wire, and now Willie's raise and the tab down at the Ryegate Bar and his daughter's new fishing pole all just made him plain angry.

Just Walk Right Out

Willie Benson watched the Musselshell River slow to a trickle that summer, the carp and bullhead twisting in the mud, the cattle tromping down to suck hot, stagnant water. Then, in August, there was no water. Sometimes, if Willie was riding fence along the dirt bed of the river, he'd talk to the cattle. He'd tell them that it had all gone dry, even the good well in town out back of the Ryegate Bar, and there wasn't a thing to do about it—*I'd get on out if I were you, just walk right out of this valley.*

Twelve Kinds of Rock

Wade Newman made his X on the calendar in the kitchen. Another rainless day. The drought was nearing a decade long, and at the Ryegate Bar they kept a list of all the ranchers along the Musselshell who had gone bankrupt or sold out since '83: the Feeneys, the Wilsons, old Tom Hougen, the Merediths and their boys, Wilbur Poole. The list went on for a couple of pages, but no one had the heart to read it all the way through. Wade was always a little anxious when Russ would pull the pages from behind the dusty row of high-priced whiskey and add another name. That fall, still waiting for rain, Wade had a fellow come in and drill a five-thousand foot well. They broke four drill bits and went through twelve kinds of rock and never hit water.

Grasshopper Dance

Jackie Newman was six years old when her father took over the RL and the family moved into the main house. She had thought moving would be an adventure, like when her father used to take her to the Ryegate Bar with him. He'd hold the door for her, and they'd walk right up front where her father hooked her by her armpits and swung her up onto one of the bar stools, and she could see all the pretty bottles ambered with liquor and see them in the mirror too. Then Russ, his bald head gleaming in the bar lights, would fish a pickle out of the glass jar on the shelf and hand it to her wrapped in a napkin. She'd spin on the stool and taste the salt and sour of the pickle and listen to the rumble of her father's laughter. The men at the bar, even the old man with the beard that lived out north, would smile at her and give her dimes and nickels for the jukebox. Eventually, as her father talked louder and longer, she would slip off the stool and sneak out the front door and follow stray cats down the alley or do a grasshopper dance in the lit ring of a streetlight. But the main house wasn't the adventure she thought it would be. Uncle Junior was always spilling his Pepsi and yelling if you changed the channel. Her mother had her doing chores day and night. And anymore her father seldom took her into town with him—there was always a drought, and he was busy with the ranch. Now, home from school and cleaning up after everyone had eaten dinner, Jackie ran the back of her hand across her forehead. She walked out the front door and sat on the steps, in the cool of the evening, the branches of the cottonwoods shifting above her in the wind. She could see Willie Benson raising dust as he ran a green broke horse hard around the ring of the corral. Her father had caught Willie napping when he was supposed to be fixing fence a few weeks ago and had him working near the house these days, just to keep an eye on him. Jackie didn't mind. Willie was good with horses, and she liked to watch him ride. Willie circled and circled, and Jackie saw the setting sun and shadow slip across his face in time.

After All

Willie Benson turned on his lamp and sat at the old desk in the bunkhouse. It was Sunday evening. The first cold wind of the season had blown in from the north that morning. Most of the other cowboys were asleep, but Willie sat thinking, pencil in his hand. He'd been writing to his mother ever since he moved in with the Newmans, and now he put his pencil to the paper Vera had given him and explained to her about his thumb and the dry river and how he wouldn't be going to Great Falls after all. When he was done, he folded the sheet of paper and put it in an envelope and licked it shut. He turned it over and carefully wrote the last address he had for his mother on the front. He'd gotten a jokey card with five bucks in it from her a few years ago, but she hadn't even signed it.

Bone Skinny

Wade Newman was on the phone in the kitchen. Jackie was watching TV with Junior in the front room. She heard her father begin to swear softly. Then he got louder. Then her mother was there telling Wade to just calm down. But he kept yelling into the phone, asking what was he supposed to do when half the wheat crop was burnt to cinders in the fields, asking how he was supposed to sell cattle that had gone bone skinny in the sun. He slammed the phone down and looked his wife in the face and told her that the operating loan might not come through from the bank in Billings this fall, that they might not be able to buy next spring's seed or even winter hay. He grabbed his truck keys and clattered out the screen door, and Jackie knew her father would come home whiskey drunk and stinking from the Ryegate Bar. She looked up and saw Junior's straw had swung the other way and was pointing at the TV. Junior craned his neck out from his wheelchair, but he was strapped in and couldn't get there. He began to grunt and mumble, and Jackie stood and turned the long straw back around in the soda can and set the tip of it between his open lips.

Bottle for the Road

Willie Benson turned twenty-one on the first of October, so Wade Newman gave all the cowboys the day off to celebrate. Willie's buddies, still calling him Stumpy, took him to the Ryegate Bar early in the morning. They ate eggs and hashbrowns and dropped double shots of whiskey into glasses of fizzy beer and sucked them down. Willie got sick before noon but kept drinking. He broke a pool stick, and Russ refused to sell him any more liquor. Willie cussed him out. Then he cussed his father, Tracy's Trucker Lounge, and Wade Newman. He broke a bottle of beer on his boot heel and swung the ragged neck of it around. Russ told him he was going to call Dejagher. Willie's friends were nervous. They got hold of Willie and put him in the truck. They bought a bottle for the road, and left.

Something Else Altogether

Jackie Newman smiled at Willie Benson and told him she thought his story about the mountains had been just wonderful. And considering how he was always reading and she was having trouble in English, she thought maybe he could help her out a bit. She smiled up at him, and Willie had to look away, look down and slap the dust from his jeans. He'd been taking Jackie out fishing ever since her mother would let her, but this felt like something else altogether. He watched the wind roll through Jackie's long, dark hair and told her he'd be happy to. She laughed, said thanks, and ran back up to the main house. Willie watched her disappear behind the door, then waved down the other cowboys and jumped in the back of the pickup for the trip to the Ryegate Bar.

Another Message with the Bank

Wade Newman sent each of his cowboys out early in the morning and told them to be back by sundown—*it's gonna be cold as a well digger's ass tonight, supposed to snow, and I'm buying whichever cowboy finds that bunch of strays a steak dinner at the Ryegate Bar tonight!* After the cowboys left, Wade tried to busy himself out in the shed, replacing blades on one of the combines and testing the belts, but after lunch he couldn't help himself. He left another message with the bank, then sat in his office, got out the calculator and all the receipts, and tried again to get it all to balance.

Far Enough

Willie Benson rode north. He found a section of the fence down and all afternoon followed a dry creek toward the mountains. Early December, biting cold. The wind coming at him in curves and circles. Yet the sun was brilliant with the sky. He rode and watched the shadows of sage and greasewood slide east, begin to stretch and twist. Ahead, farther north, the Snowy Mountains went blue-black, a shade darker than the darkening sky. As the sun disappeared, Willie studied the up-sloping land, the black rocks and the pines. He realized Great Falls must be just over these mountains, though for the shadows and the wind, he wasn't sure how close he was, just how far he'd come. He knew he'd come a long ways, but he didn't know how far was far enough. The cold was dark and hard. He thought about the old wood stove in corner of the Ryegate Bar. He tried to shake the pain from his hand. It didn't leave. There was just wind, a seam of scar, then bone.

All the Way to the Mountains

Jackie Newman watched the heavy flakes of snow dance into the circle of light the lamp threw out the window, then dance back to darkness. Earlier that evening she had taken her homework down to the bunkhouse, but the other cowboys, all getting ready to drive to the Ryegate Bar, told her Willie was still out looking for the strays. As the night blackened she thought about leaving her books on the kitchen table and saddling her horse and riding out through the soft falling snow of the valley and up into the north wind cracking across the high plain that she believed, for she had never ridden much farther than the river, rolled all the way to the mountains. But she didn't go. Jackie just stared out the window, wondering how far Willie had gone.

A Daddy and a Thumb

Willie Benson told Wade Newman that he'd gotten lost up north, spent the night in an old homesteader's shack. Wade didn't believe him. He thought Willie'd been out drinking at the Ryegate Bar. Wade swore at him. He asked him if he didn't care about the strays, told him that the price of calves had bottomed out, that the bank called again about the operating loan, that they were running out of alfalfa hay—*this is real shit, Willie. The RL's in trouble. You can't hang dog around here cause you lost a daddy and a thumb. Hell. We all lose a daddy*—Wade stopped yelling as he saw his daughter walk up through the new snow, saw her smile at Willie. Wade told her to get on in the house.

Fast Down the Gravel Road

Jackie Newman propped her window open with her math book, held her shoes in her hand, and padded across the rooftop until she could safely jump to the ground. She met Starla Collier at the bottom of the hill, about a half mile from the house. They drove fast down the gravel road into town, wind in their hair, music metallic and loud from the tape deck, laughing through cigarettes and half a bottle of Starla's mother's peach schnapps. There were nearly a dozen pickups parked outside the Ryegate Bar, and Jackie told Starla to pull over by the little Chevy Luv her father had been letting Willie use—*I'm going to leave him a note. I want to tell him something.*

Profit and Loss

Wade Newman ate an early lunch at the Ryegate Bar and left for Billings at noon. It was March and the snow was already melting along the valley, but Wade hoped the snow still held in the mountains, along the streams that fed the Musselshell in the spring. Wade drove and drove and sat in a little chair across from a thick desk of dark red wood and talked for nearly an hour about how it was something good to raise up grain, fat cattle, and a family, about how hard his daddy had worked and the money he'd invested at this very bank and how rich the land along the Musselshell Valley was when the river ran. He told the bank's man that the land itself was all much more than wind and dust, river and pine, that it was beautiful, and as he said it, Wade realized he believed it all himself. But the banker leaned back in his leather chair and said that these days river and pine meant a lot less to the world than profit and loss.

Blue Neon

Willie Benson walked into the Ryegate Bar and asked for a case of beer and a bottle of vodka. Edna slid off her stool, limped to the back room, her shoes scraping the raw boards of the floor. She hauled out a case of Budweiser and limped back. She scooted an ashtray out of the way and set the case on the pine wood. The bottles clanked. Willie packed his Copenhagen, his loose finger popping the can. Edna pulled a key from around her neck and bent to the locked liquor cabinet beneath the bar. Willie heard the small grind of the gears and pinched a wad of chew and shoved it in his lip, then wiped his fingers on the ass of his jeans. Edna straightened, cursed her shrunken leg, and held the vodka bottle out to Willie. He dropped some greasy bills on the bar and took the bottle. She counted out all the ones and fives and went to make change, but Willie told her not to bother. He tucked the bottle of vodka into his armpit and loaded the case of beer into his arms. Edna asked if he needed anything else. Willie grinned, and Edna saw blue neon light in his gray eyes—he told her thanks, but he was doing all right. Edna could feel the weather in the gnarled bones of her hip, the ice on the river would break early this year and the spring sap would soon rise in the trees. Edna had married Matt Crandall right here in the bar nearly forty years ago, when she was fourteen, and she figured Willie Benson was buying beer for some high school kids. Probably Jackie Newman she thought—*Wade had better watch that cowboy.*

The First Stars

Jackie Newman drove one of her father's farm trucks up the gravel of Main Street and back down. Other cars full of teenagers circled the same dusty track, flashing their lights and yelling and laughing. But Jackie didn't pay any attention to them. She kept her eyes on the wood door of the Ryegate Bar. She was anxious and excited to pick up Willie, drop the pedal to the floor, and head out of town. Her father had been in Billings all afternoon and when her mother left for a church meeting, she had taken the truck without permission. She hooked her left arm out the window and watched the white glow in the north join the first stars in the night sky. The northern lights, she thought, but then Willie Benson kicked the bar door open, and she turned the wheel hard.

The Names

Wade Newman knew his father had set up half the households in the county with a grubstake. They had all come off the trains in the forties, half blind in the baking sun, and stumbled down Main Street Ryegate where they ran into wiry young Robert Newman, who put them to work feeding cattle and knocking wheat down. A few years later, when they left the RL with their skin callused, their muscles worked lean and hard, most of them carried a big enough chunk of money to buy their own piece of the Musselshell Valley. Wade turned his truck onto Main Street and pulled up in front of the Ryegate Bar. It was late, and Wade sat a bit and wondered if Vera was home from her church meeting, if maybe she wouldn't ask and he could just sit in the front room and watch television with Junior. No, he thought. He wouldn't go home and cry with his wife or sit with his cripple of a brother tonight. He killed the engine and stepped out of the truck. The sky pulsed with light, brighter than the neon beer signs in the window. Wade had only seen the aurora borealis this wild and bright once before, when he was a small child. He pushed open the door of the Ryegate Bar and took a long look at all the men whose fathers his father had built, then walked slowly toward the bar, his boots grinding down on the sawdust scattered across the floor. He sat down and asked for a shot of whiskey with a beer back. He told Russ to bring him the list—*I want to see them all. The names.*

Lightning Run the Wrong Way

Willie Benson told her he loved her. And Jackie Newman said that was nice, but she still wasn't going to take off her panties. It was near midnight, and they were laid out on Willie's bedroll on top of Rig Butte, Willie in his blue jeans, Jackie in her underwear, the wind cold along the lengths of their bodies. They could hear the rumbling black hammers of the rigs pulling oil, the distant roar of diesel trucks making time down Highway 12. And fire dazzled the dark sky—blue lightning run the wrong way, red eruptions and the slow fade to gold, a white ache along the horizon. He told her that he had ridden too far, that he had ridden right into the mountains and been lost and cold. Then he'd seen an old shack with a lit window. He'd knocked on the door, and the old man from the Ryegate Bar, Caleb Meyer, had answered.

Never Rain

Wade Newman was drunk, the flesh of his face shiny and slack, his eyes far-away. He put his hand around a bottle of beer and told Russ Crandall that it must be the devil drinking the river dry each spring. He said maybe his crackpot brother, Franklin, was right, maybe the Lord was angry, watching the good dust of the fields blow to heaven, sending wind and wind and never rain. Russ clucked his tongue, wiped his hands on his apron. Wade looked up at him and told him he needed just enough to get the alfalfa planted, then he could coast through summer until the calves sold in September—*enough to get the hay in the ground, Russ. I know my daddy helped you get the bar started, and he told me if I was ever in a tight spot to ask you. He said, 'Russ'll help you.' Well, I'm asking here.* Russ worried his apron some more. He told Wade he couldn't do it. Said times were tough and a guy had to watch his investments, but not to worry about the beer—*it's on the house.*

A Sudden Rose

Jackie Newman stood up, the slender curve of her hips straightening. The sky went a sudden rose, and Willie told her he was a man now, twenty-one. He told her they were old enough, could be together. He told her he would go down to the Ryegate Bar right now and tell Wade they were in love and leaving this dry land and he couldn't do anything about it. Jackie had never heard anyone talk about living somewhere else and mean it. Though it was hard for her to imagine what it might be like, she loved the sound of it. She winged her arms back and undid her bra. She slid her panties down her hips and lightly stepped out of them.

Spring Snow

Vera Newman watched the April sky swirl with snow. Willie and Jackie had been missing for nearly a week. Wade had gone into a rage those first days, a warrant out for Willie and curses for them both. But he stayed in bed today. So Vera made breakfast for the cowboys, told them to do up the day's chores. She went through Jackie's room and called Tim Dejagher half a dozen times. She brought Wade a vitamin and a glass of water, told him Franklin had called. She let the cowboys take the rest of the day off and go on in to the Ryegate Bar. She asked them to let her know if they heard anything. She wheeled Junior into the front room and together they watched the spring snow.

Her Mind Gone to Wind and Pines

Caleb Meyer saw them ride up in the snow. He knew the boy from the Ryegate Bar. He had never seen the girl. She was slender, very young, her face smooth as river stone. They said they needed a place to stay out the storm. He let them have the back room of the cabin and moved his bedroll up by the fire. The snow fell thick and heavy. They woke with the sun that first day, fed the chickens and the sheep, helped split wood. The boy played cribbage with him after dinner and shared the whiskey he'd brought. Caleb didn't ask why they'd come or how long they might stay. He had stories to tell. Stories he thought they should hear. He told them which rocks curl the water right for brook trout, how to trap for coyote and bobcat in the high country in the summer. He said the wild plums out east on the prairie made a fine sauce for biscuits. He told them how he built the corrals by hand. He talked about his mother, alone in the mountains, her young husband dead, her mind gone to wind and pines. He showed them the dusty trunk full of her dresses, and the girl kneeled down and opened the leather latch. She held a blue dress up to the light of the oil lamps.

Alone in the Afternoons

Willie Benson drove out from Caleb Meyer's place early in the morning. To the west, the mountains stood tall and strong, their shoulders white with snow, the sky a soft blue arc in the east. Willie was headed for the hospital in Great Falls. He figured it was June; they had been staying with Caleb for nearly two months. Jackie had turned sixteen. Caleb had smoked a mess of trout for her birthday dinner. Willie had drunk all the whiskey he'd brought from the Ryegate Bar and taken to riding up into the mountains alone in the afternoons. He knew he'd done this thing, but he didn't know if it was enough. Or if it was any good. Then Caleb had gotten sick. He was weak and chilled for a few days, just shuffling around the house wrapped in a blanket. But soon he couldn't get out of bed. For the three days it took Willie to get the ancient GMC truck parked out behind the barn working, Caleb had been delirious. Willie and Jackie loaded the old man into the cab as best they could. They held each other as the day came slowly on, saying nothing. Jackie was thinking of Caleb, of how just before he had gotten sick the two of them had pulled up the winter trapline and greased the steel joints of the traps and hung them in the dark of the shed. Willie watched her touch Caleb's ragged face through the open truck window. Then he let her go and got behind the wheel. He turned the key and heard the storm of the engine.

North up the Road

The sun was white in the sky, and the first hot winds of summer blew dust across the road. Meyer was dead, had died miles back. Willie kept driving, was still talking to the old man, telling him about the A he'd got in English for that story, the books he liked to read. He told the dead man about how the bunkhouse back at the RL smelled of pine pitch, gasoline, and bourbon. He told him how Wade Newman might lose the RL. He was quiet a moment, remembering the last he'd heard of his mother, a police report in the Billings newspaper, her blood shot full of methamphetamine. Then he told Meyer that too. And he cried, the road a sudden river. He turned east onto the hard pan sage flats and stopped on a ridge above a dry creek. His father was dead, he didn't have a thumb, the river would dry again this summer, the list down at the Ryegate Bar would grow. And Wade and Vera Newman had no idea where their sixteen-year-old daughter was. Willie Benson hauled Caleb out of the truck and carried him down to the creek bed. He laid him out in the shade of the bank and said one of Vera's prayers over the gray rag of his body. He got back in the truck. Willie Benson thought for a moment, then drove north up the road toward Great Falls.

Beautiful

Jackie Newman opened the windows to catch the cool night air. She watched the first drops of rain raise small clouds of dust. She lit one of the lamps and drank creek water from a steel cup. She had been alone for many days now. She knew Willie had left her. At first, Jackie had missed both Willie and Caleb, then she had missed driving fast over gravel roads with Starla, clearing dishes in the kitchen with her mother, and even dropping a straw in a soda can for Junior. But yesterday she pulled four brook trout from the deep pool north of the shack and laid a bowl of wild rose blossoms on the hunk of stone nestled in the crooked roots of pine that Caleb had told her was his mother's grave. She watched gray moths dance through the flickering lamplight and thought about how very different things were up here, and how very much the same. Tomorrow she would ride through the sheep to check for coyote kills and fix the corral gate. Most of the dresses in Caleb's trunk fit her just right. And even without a mirror, alone and far up in the mountains, Jackie Newman knew she was beautiful when she wore the blue one.

The Wild Smell of Rain

Wade Newman rode hard for the Snowy Mountains. The day was all but gone, the sky shot through with rose and deeper rose and blue ash. The letter from Willie had come in the mail that morning, along with the final notice from the bank, and Wade saddled up his best horse to cut straight across country, knowing that driving the only crooked road north would take him nearly twice as long. But he was still far from where the letter said his daughter would be. There was dust and the stink of sage, hot wind, then, suddenly, the wild smell of rain. Wade Newman looked to the mountains and the mass of black clouds moving out over the prairie and down the valley. He said the word into the wind. He said it again—*rain*.

Back Behind the Bar

Edna Crandall wiped down the wood lip of the bar and listened to rain ring on the tin roof. It had been ten years since they'd had a good spring storm, and the men would be in soon, buying beers and slapping each other on the back. It got louder and louder, and Edna left her towel and limped to the window. Main Street ran with mud and water, the world rain gray twenty feet out. Edna had been fifty-four years in this place, and at first she thought she had seen it come down like this before, once a very long time ago. But the longer she stood there, the more it seemed she had never seen such rain. Still, she couldn't be sure, and she didn't like being confused about things, so she hobbled back behind the bar and waited.